Max and Zoe

at the Dentist

3 1389 02074 8232

by Shelley Swanson Sateren

illustrated by Mary Sullivan

PICTURE WINDOW BOOKS
a capstone imprint

Max and Zoe is published by Picture Window Books
a Capstone Imprint
151 Good Counsel Drive, P.O. Box 669
Mankato, Minnesota 56002
www.capstonepub.com

Library of Congress Cataloging-in-Publication Data
Sateren, Shelley Swanson.
  Max and Zoe at the dentist / by Shelley Swanson Sateren ; illustrated by Mary Sullivan.
     p. cm. -- (Max and Zoe)
  Summary: Zoe helps Max feel brave when he has to go to the dentist to have two teeth pulled.
  ISBN 978-1-4048-6206-7 (library binding)
  [1. Dentists--Fiction. 2. Friendship--Fiction.] I. Sullivan, Mary, 1958- ill. II. Title.
  PZ7.S249155Mar 2011
  [E]--dc22
                    2011006482

Art Director: Kay Fraser
Designer: Emily Harris

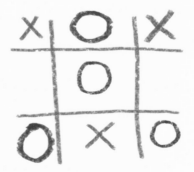

Printed in the United States of America in Melrose Park, Illinois.   032011   006112LKF11

1/1"

Table of Contents

Chapter 1
Problem Teeth

It was time for Buddy's walk. Max and Zoe grabbed his leash.

"I'm scared, Zoe," Max said.

"I would be, too. Show me your teeth again," Zoe said.

Max opened his mouth.

He pointed to the problem teeth.

"It's these baby ones on the bottom. They get pulled out tomorrow," Max said.

"Do they have to?" Zoe asked.

"Yeah. My mom said they have to so my grown-up teeth will come in straight," Max said with a frown.

Suddenly, a
squirrel ran by.

Buddy yanked hard
on the leash. Max
almost fell over!

Buddy pulled Max down the
street. Zoe raced to keep up.

"I bet this is how hard the dentist will pull. I bet it will really hurt!" Max said.

"You just have to be brave," said Zoe. "We have the same dentist. He gives cool prizes. I got a toy hammer and screwdriver."

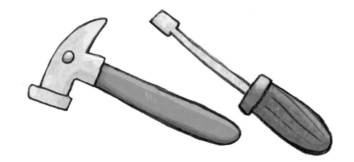

"Well, he could give me two hundred dollars," said Max. "The tooth fairy could, too. And it still wouldn't be enough!"

Chapter 2

Beyond Brave

The next day, Max hid

under a chair. He was in the

waiting room at the dentist's

office.

Mom poked him. "Come

out, Max," she said.

"No way. I want to talk

to Zoe," Max said.

Mom gave Max her

phone. He called Zoe.

"Hi. It's me, Max."

"Hey!" Zoe said.

"Remember to pick different tools for prizes. Then we'll have the whole set! Be brave!"

"Um, okay," Max said.

Max wished it were over. He wanted to go home.

"If only I had the tools

right now," he thought.

"Then maybe I'd feel better."

Max stuck out his head.

"Can I get my prizes first?"

he asked the helper.

"Of course!" she said. She
came back with the box of
prizes.

Max picked his tools, then
he crawled out.

"Okay. I'm ready now,"
he said.

Max held the toys super tight and walked to the dentist chair.

"Here we go," said the dentist. "First, I'll give you a shot. Then you won't feel anything when I pull out the teeth."

The shot hurt a little. Now Max couldn't feel his mouth. It felt strange. He shut his eyes.

"Take deep breaths," said the dentist.

Max did. Then he felt a

tug inside his mouth.

"There!" said the dentist.

"One is out."

"What?" thought Max.

"Already?"

Max felt another tug.

"We are

done!" the

dentist said.

"Really?" thought Max.

"That was so fast! And it

hardly hurt!"

The helper gave Max

a tiny box. His teeth were

inside.

"I did it, Mom! I feel so brave!" Max said.

"Max, you were beyond brave," his mom said.

Chapter 3
The Best Part

After the dentist, Mom

drove to the grocery store.

"You need to eat soft

foods, Max. Have fun

picking out whatever you

want," she said.

Max loaded the cart with
applesauce, ice cream, and
soup.

"This is the best part!"
he said.

That night, Max put the

teeth under his pillow.

"You did great today,"

said Mom. "Maybe the tooth

fairy will bring you extra

money."

In the morning, Max found money under his pillow.

"Wow! This is the best part!" he said.

That afternoon, Zoe came over. They played with their new tool set.

"I was wrong again," Max said. "THIS is definitely the best part!"

About the Author

Shelley Swanson Sateren is the author of many children's books and has worked as an editor and a bookseller. Today, besides writing, she works with children aged five to twelve in an after-school program. At home or at the cabin, Shelley loves to read, watch movies, cross-country ski, and walk. She lives in St. Paul, Minnesota, with her husband and two sons.

About the Illustrator

Mary Sullivan has been drawing and writing her whole life, which has mostly been spent in Texas. She earned her BFA from the University of Texas in Studio Art, but she considers herself a self-trained illustrator. Mary lives in Cedar Park, a suburb of Austin, Texas.

Glossary

brave (BRAVE) — to show courage

definitely (DEF-uh-nit-lee) — with certainty

dentist (DEN-tist) — someone who is trained to check, clean, and treat teeth

leash (LEESH) — a rope used to hold and control an animal

office (AU-fiss) — a room or building where people work

prize (PRIZE) — something you get for winning a game or for doing something good

Discussion Questions

1. Why is it important to go to the dentist?

2. At first, Max felt scared. Then he felt brave. Talk about a time when you felt brave.

3. When Max felt scared, he called Zoe. Who would you call if you felt scared? Why?

Writing Prompts

1. Write one sentence about what you like about the dentist. Then write one sentence about what you don't like about the dentist.

2. Make a grocery list of five foods that you would pick after having a tooth pulled. Remember, they need to be soft foods.

3. Would you want to be a dentist? Write down your answer and your reason.

Hi MAX!

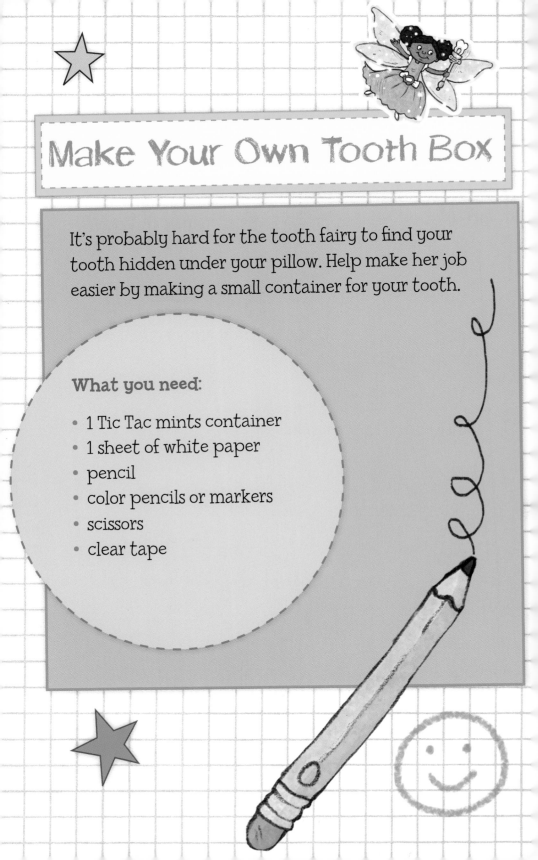

Make Your Own Tooth Box

It's probably hard for the tooth fairy to find your tooth hidden under your pillow. Help make her job easier by making a small container for your tooth.

What you need:

- 1 Tic Tac mints container
- 1 sheet of white paper
- pencil
- color pencils or markers
- scissors
- clear tape

What you do:

1. Lay the Tic Tac container on the paper and trace the shape.

2. Cut out the rectangle shape you traced.

3. Decorate the rectangle. Feel free to use stickers, markers, etc. You could even write a short message to the tooth fairy.

4. Tape the paper onto the container.

5. When you lose a tooth, put it inside the box and put it under your pillow.

The tooth fairy will be able to see your tooth through the clear sides of the box!

The Fun Doesn't Stop Here!

Discover more at www.capstonekids.com

- Videos & Contests
- Games & Puzzles
- Friends & Favorites
- Authors & Illustrators

Find cool websites and more books like this one at www.facthound.com. Just type in the Book ID **9781404862067** and you're ready to go!